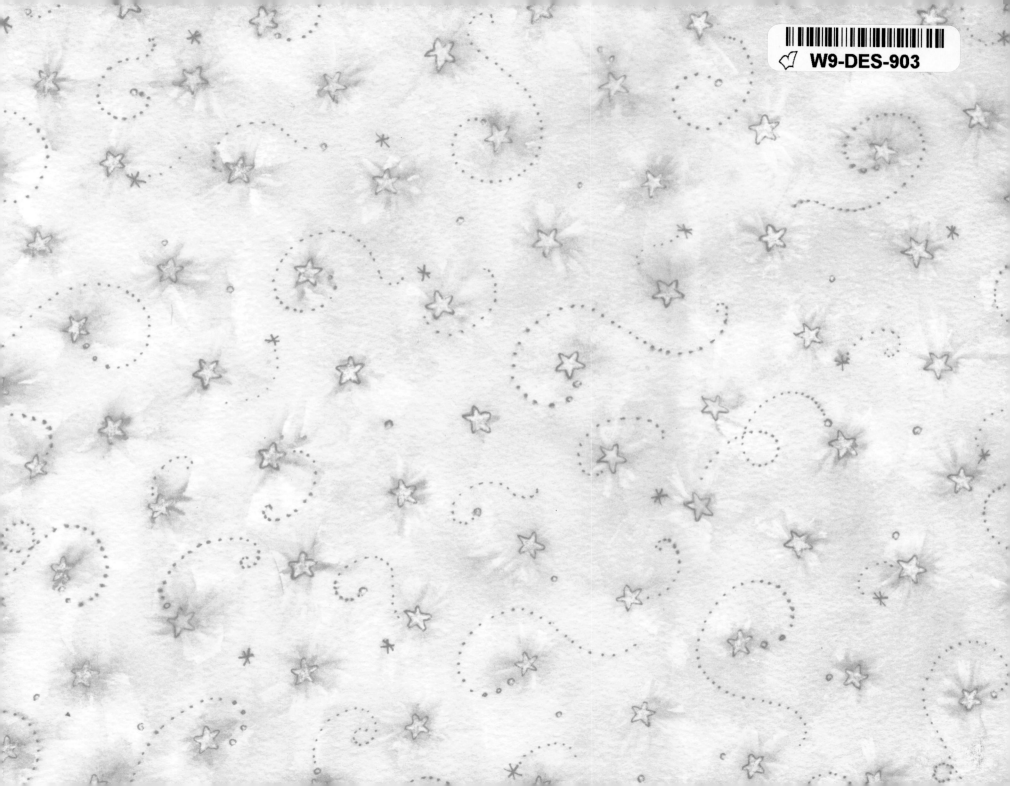

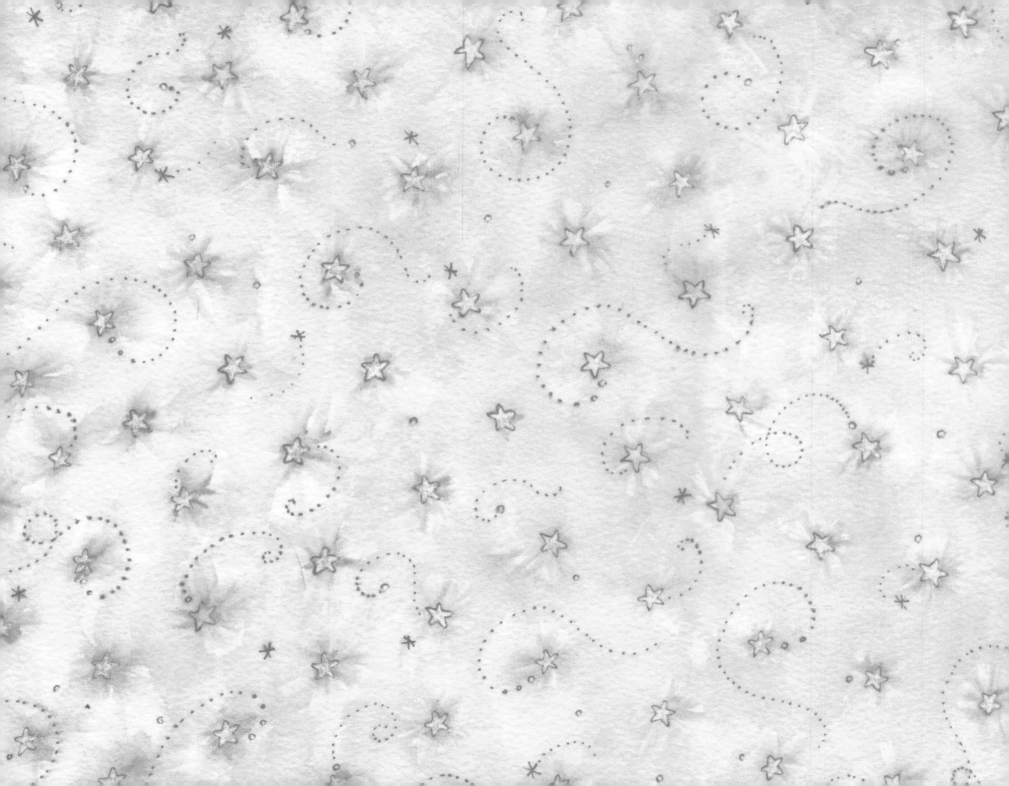

THE BELLY BUTTON FAIRY

BOOK AND AUDIO CD

BY BOBBIE HINMAN

ILLUSTRATED BY MARK WAYNE ADAMS

DESIGN AND LAYOUT BY JEFF URBANCIC

Every belly has a button!
Bobbie Hinman
2009

Best Fairy Books

www.bestfairybooks.com

The Belly Button Fairy

Copyright © 2009 Bobbie Hinman
Illustrations by Mark Wayne Adams

Voices on CD: Narrator, Bobbie Hinman; Guitar and vocals, Nelson Emokpae;
Chorus, Bobbie's grandchildren and friends - Jordan, Kaitlyn, Emily, Lindsay, Leah, Katya and Erin

Text design and layout: Jeff Urbancic
Audio engineer: William Whiteford

Library of Congress Control Number: 2008908155

Publisher's Cataloging-in-Publication
(Provided by Quality Books, Inc.)

Hinman, Bobbie.
  The belly button fairy / by Bobbie Hinman ;
illustrated by Mark Wayne Adams.
    p. cm.
    SUMMARY: In this rhyming story, a grandmotherly fairy
flies through the skies in her rocking chair, carrying a
ruler and a bucket of fairy dust. She is responsible for
making sure that every child has a belly button, and
that it's "always in the middle."
    ISBN-13: 978-0-9786791-3-2
    ISBN-10: 0-9786791-3-X

    1. Fairies–Juvenile fiction. 2. Navel–Juvenile
fiction. [1. Fairies–Fiction. 2. Belly button–
Fiction. 3. Stories in rhyme.]   I. Adams, Mark Wayne, ill.
II. Title.

PZ8.3.H5564Bel 2009   [E]
                    QBI08-600248

For information: www.bestfairybooks.com

This book is dedicated with love to every child who has a belly button.
And to my precious grandchildren.
Tickle, tickle, tickle!

Do you believe in fairies who flitter around at all hours?

And one more question. . . do you believe that fairies have magical powers?

Now I think this is real. Oh, I think this is true.

Yes, it happened to me and it happened to you.

Take a look in the mirror. Do you see something funny?

Is there a round hole right there on your tummy?

Now listen my friends, and I'll tell you, I will...

just how that hole got there. Now sit very still.

Once upon a time, as I was lying on my bed,

I heard a fairy talking, and this is what she said...

"My dear, I think you're very cute. You are. But bless my soul!

In the middle of your tummy is a funny little hole!"

Then she told me how it happened while she sat there on my bed.

"I'm the Belly Button Fairy!" is exactly what she said.

She said, "Every belly has a button.

Some are big and some are little."

"But one thing always stays the same...

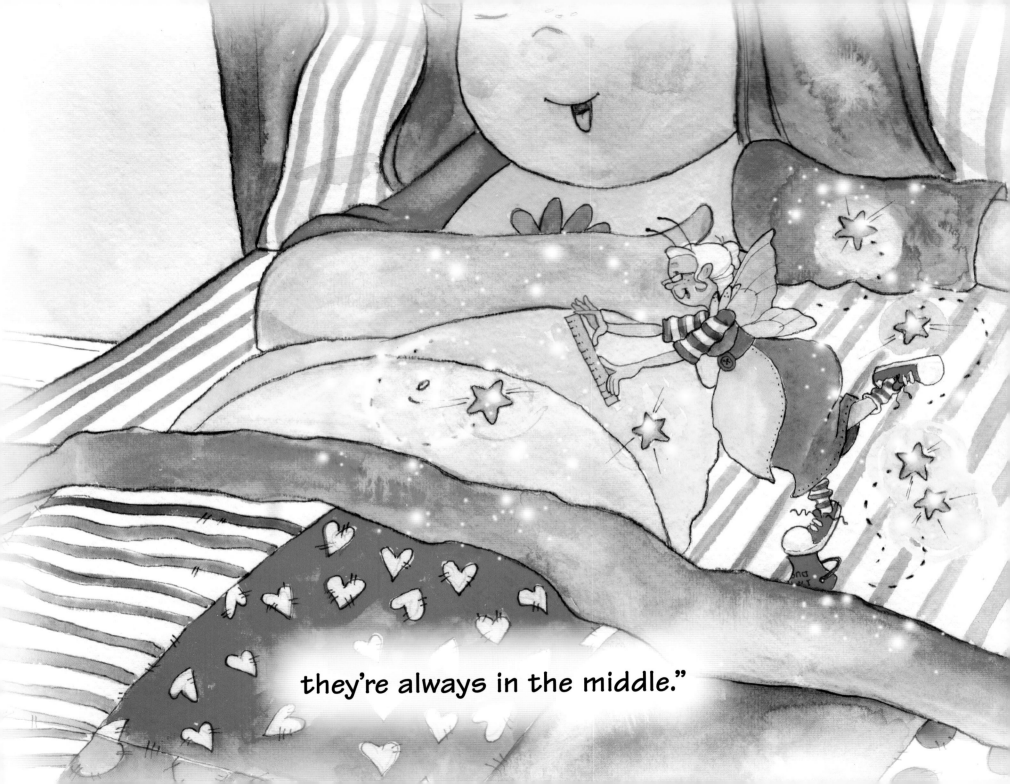

they're always in the middle."

She said, "Some buttons may turn in, while others may turn out.

But each of us has only one. There isn't any doubt."

She said she sneaks into the hospital very late at night...

and sprinkles bits of fairy dust at just the perfect height.

Then she lines up all the babies,

one after another...

and says, "You're done! You're done! You're done!

Now, where's your sister or brother?"

Then before she flies away at night she says, "Now I can see...

I've made you oh so perfect. Thumbs up if you agree!"

The Belly Button Fairy Song
(To the tune of Yankee Doodle)

Verse 1.
I see something in the sky.
There's no need to be wary.
Flying in her rocking chair
Is the belly button fairy.

Chorus
Belly buttons in or out,
May be big or little.
One thing always stays the same,
They're always in the middle.

Verse 2.
Look into the mirror and
You may see something funny.
Is there a silly little hole
In the middle of your tummy?

Chorus
Belly buttons in or out,
May be big or little.
One thing always stays the same,
They're always in the middle.

Verse 3.
She sprinkles bits of fairy dust
On every little baby.
Now do you think she's really real?
The answer friends is ... maybe.

Chorus
Belly buttons in or out,
May be big or little.
One thing always stays the same,
They're always in the middle.

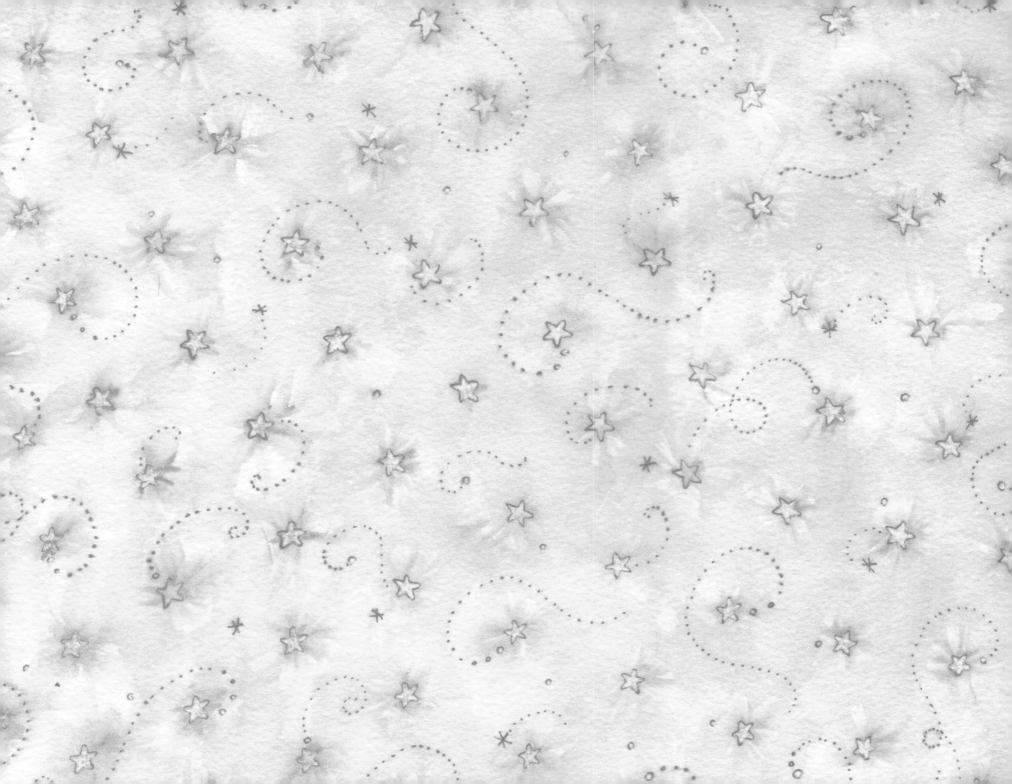

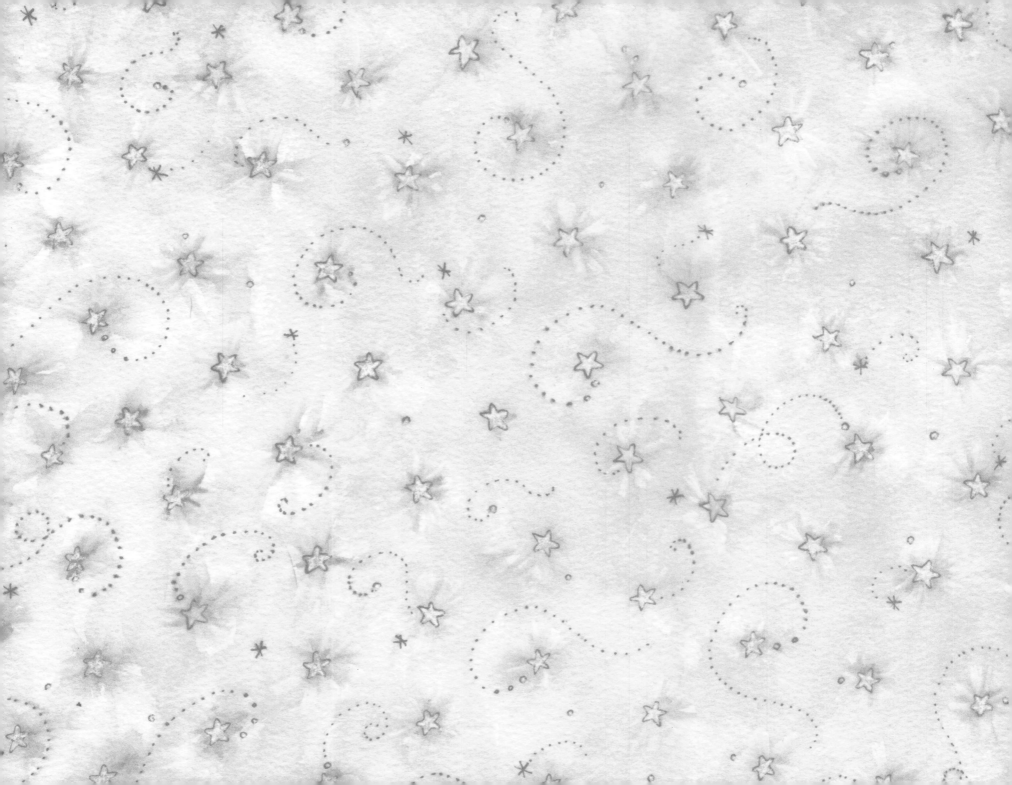